RAM

Detroit Pistons

Richard Rambeck

CREATIVE EDUCATION

Published by Creative Education
123 South Broad Street, Mankato, Minnesota 56001
Creative Education is an imprint of The Creative Company

Designed by Rita Marshall

Photos by: Allsport Photography, Associated Press/Wide World Photos, Focus on Sports, NBA Photos, UPI/Corbis-Bettmann, and SportsChrome.

Photo page 1: Isiah Thomas
Photo title page: Terry Mills

Copyright © 1998 Creative Education.
International copyrights reserved in all countries.
No part of this book may be reproduced in any form without written permission from the publisher.
Printed in the United States of America.

Library of Congress Cataloging-in-Publication Data

Rambeck, Richard.
Detroit Pistons / Richard Rambeck.
p. cm. — (NBA today)
Summary: Describes the background and history of the Detroit Pistons pro basketball team to 1997.
ISBN 0-88682-873-2

1. Detroit Pistons (Basketball team)—History—Juvenile literature.
[1. Detroit Pistons (Basketball team)—History. 2. Basketball—History.]
I. Title. II. Series: NBA today (Mankato, Minn.)

GV885.52.D47R36 1997   96-6535
796.323'64'0977434—dc21

First edition

5 4 3 2 1

D etroit, once a tiny French fort and trading village, is now one of the largest cities in the United States. Located near Lake Erie, the city is a major international port. Goods are shipped from Detroit, through the Great Lakes, and up the St. Lawrence Seaway.

But Detroit is best known as the automobile capital of the United States. The city is home to the Big Three automakers—Ford, General Motors, and Chrysler—and is known as the "Motor City." The connection between Detroit and the auto industry is so strong that some car models are even named after people who helped shape the city's history. In

Walter Dukes was an early Pistons star.

Led by guard Fred Schaus, the Fort Wayne Pistons posted a 40–28 record in their first NBA season.

1701, for example, a man named Antoine Cadillac founded the French trading village that eventually became the city of Detroit. And in 1760, an Indian war chief named Pontiac attacked that village. These two men played important roles in the city's history, and their names—Cadillac and Pontiac—now adorn vehicles around the world.

It's not surprising, then, that Detroit is home to the only professional sports team named after a part of a car—the Detroit Pistons, members of the National Basketball Association (NBA) since 1957. What is surprising is that the Pistons didn't start out in Detroit. The franchise first played in Fort Wayne, Indiana. The Fort Wayne Pistons were among the original members of the National Basketball Association when the league was formed in 1949.

It took 40 years and one change of address for the Detroit Pistons to capture their first NBA title. Led by guards Isiah Thomas and Joe Dumars, the Pistons won the 1989 championship. A year later, the team repeated its success and captured the 1990 league championship as well. The Pistons gave the Detroit fans plenty to cheer about during those two magical seasons, and today with Grant Hill, Grant Long, and ageless Joe Dumars, they hope the magic will return.

FROM FORT WAYNE TO THE MOTOR CITY

When the NBA was formed, the Fort Wayne Pistons were among the league's more colorful franchises. The club's owner, Fred Zollner, had first put together the team in 1937 to play in a local industrial league. Zollner owned a large factory that made pistons for automobiles,

Veteran rebounder Otis Thorpe.

George Yardley was the first NBA player to score 2,000 points in a season.

which explains how the team got its name. The Fort Wayne Pistons joined the National Basketball League (NBL), one of the earliest pro organizations, in 1941. The team soon rose to the top of the NBL, winning league titles in both 1944 and 1945. But when the NBL merged with another league to form the NBA in 1949, the Pistons stopped running so smoothly. They usually finished third or fourth in the NBA's Western Division.

The club's luck changed for the better in 1954–55. Zollner surprised everyone by hiring a former NBA referee, Charlie Eckman, to coach the team. Eckman directed stars Max Zaslofsky, Andy Phillip, Frank Brian, and George Yardley to a 43–29 record and a first-place finish in the Western Division. Then the Pistons powered past the Minneapolis Lakers in the playoffs to reach the NBA finals. The club's title run ended there, however. In an exciting seven-game series, Fort Wayne was edged out by the Syracuse Nationals for the league championship. The final game of that series went right down to the wire. In the closing seconds, the Nats' George King sank a free throw to break a 91–91 tie, and then stole the ball to assure a 92–91 Syracuse victory.

The following year, the Pistons again topped the Western Division, and again, they reached the championship round of the playoffs, only to lose to Philadelphia.

The fans in Fort Wayne were delighted with their team, but Fred Zollner knew that such a small city could not give the Pistons the support they needed to survive. So Zollner said goodbye to the citizens of Fort Wayne and moved the team to Detroit. While Zollner's players now had more fans to cheer them on, the Pistons struggled for success throughout their first decade in the Motor City.

The early Detroit teams were built around guard Gene Shue, forward Bailey Howell, and a youngster named Dave DeBusschere, a native of Detroit. DeBusschere, who played both guard and forward, was a fine scorer, but he was better known for his great defense and rebounding skills. He also had a great basketball mind. In fact, the Pistons were so impressed with DeBusschere's intelligence that they made him a player/coach in 1964. DeBusschere—who had also pitched for the Chicago White Sox for several seasons—was only 24 years old when he took over the Pistons' coaching duties.

Dave DeBusschere pitched 83 innings for the Chicago White Sox and then played 80 games with the Pistons.

DeBusschere had good statistics as a player, but his coaching record was poor. The Pistons were among the least successful teams in the NBA, tying with the New York Knicks for the worst record in the league during the 1965–66 season. The Knicks and Pistons flipped a coin to decide which team would get the first pick in the 1966 draft. Every Detroit fan wanted the Pistons to get that first choice and take University of Michigan star Cazzie Russell. But the Pistons lost the coin flip. The Knicks made Russell the first pick in the draft, and Detroit settled for a 6-foot-2 guard from Syracuse University named Dave Bing.

BING RINGS IN SEVERAL SUCCESSFUL SEASONS

When he first came to Detroit, Dave Bing knew that many Pistons fans were disappointed that he, and not local hero Cazzie Russell, was the team's newest star. But Bing didn't let that bother him. He played brilliantly, scoring

Dave Bing, a superstar of the '70s.

Mark Aguirre, a standout in the '80s.

Ray Scott netted a total of 323 free throws to lead the Detroit Pistons.

20 points a game and earning the NBA Rookie of the Year award in his initial season. The following year, he was even better. Although Bing wasn't a great outside shooter, Pistons coach Dennis Butcher, who took over the club midway through Bing's rookie season, knew the slim guard was the best offensive weapon the team had. "I told him that if I'm going to play him 40 to 45 minutes a game, he has to take 35 shots a game," Butcher explained.

Bing listened to his coach, and wound up putting enough shots in to average 27.1 points a game. That was good enough to earn him the 1967–68 NBA scoring title, making Bing the only Piston to ever top the league in that category. He also was the first guard in 20 years to lead the league in scoring. "He's going to be a lot greater than I thought he

The talented Otto Moore (20) and Dave Bing (21).

would," Butcher said. "I don't think he's got all of his ability out fully. He'll just get better and better."

Bing's play also won over the rest of the NBA. "You can't open up a man's chest and look at his heart," said Boston coach Red Auerbach. "But I guarantee there's one big one beating in Bing. Give me one man like Dave Bing, and I'll build a championship team around him."

Unfortunately, the Pistons never managed to do that. They did make the playoffs after the 1967–68 season, but the team took a giant step backward in the middle of the next season when DeBusschere was traded to the New York Knicks. DeBusschere went on to become one of the key members of two championship teams for the Knicks. Meanwhile, the Pistons struggled along, at the bottom of the NBA standings.

After seven seasons, Eddie Miles, a one-time leading scorer, left for Baltimore.

LANIER LANDS BIG IN THE MOTOR CITY

Detroit took a big step forward in the 1970 college draft when it selected the 6-foot-11, 275-pound center, Bob Lanier. Lanier was not only a powerful player, he also had an excellent shooting touch. Opponents couldn't believe it when Lanier threw his weight around near the basket and then stepped outside and hit 15-foot jump shots.

Lanier's calling card, though, was his strength. He made sure that opponents knew how powerful he was. "I was well aware of Bob's great strength," said Cleveland center Steve Patterson. "But I went there and leaned on him anyway. I mean I hammered him, and I practically hung on him. Then, all of a sudden, he just wrapped his arm around me and threw me to the ground like I was made of straw. To tell the

Jimmy Walker's 397 free throws set a team high for the second year in a row.

truth, I still don't know how he did it. I knew right away that Bob wasn't trying to hurt me. He was the first one over to give me a hand and help me to my feet."

Lanier added muscle to the Pistons attack, and the team made great strides. Detroit finished the 1970–71 season with a 45–37 record—the club's best mark since it had moved to the Motor City. The Pistons had major injury problems the next season, however, and failed to make the playoffs. New coach Ray Scott built the team back up. Scott coached the Pistons to a franchise-best record of 52–30 during the 1973–74 season and was named NBA Coach of the Year.

Scott refused to take any credit for the team's success. "A coach is only as good as his players," Scott would often say. During the 1974–75 season, when Bob Lanier was hobbled by a series of injuries, the Pistons and their coach believed they were only as good as their giant center. Lanier had tendinitis and arthritis in his left knee. Every few days his knee had to be drained of fluid. Lanier packed his knee in ice after every game to reduce the pain and swelling.

While Lanier was icing his wounds, his teammates paid him compliment after compliment. Forward Curtis Rowe called Lanier the Pistons' "savior." Forward Don Adams said the big center was the team's "healer." Bing explained that Lanier was "our leader." "Listen to those guys," Lanier chuckled. "They think I'm Moses."

"Moses" Lanier led the Pistons to the playoffs in 1974–75, but it was to be the team's last good season for a long time. The Pistons lost to Seattle in the first round of the playoffs, and then said farewell to Dave Bing, who was traded to the Washington Bullets after the season ended. "How do you say

Hall of Famer Bob Lanier.

Second-year Piston Chris Ford led the team in steals the first of four seasons.

goodbye to someone like that?" moaned Ray Scott after the loss of Bing, who would eventually be named, along with Lanier, to the Basketball Hall of Fame. Scott soon said goodbye to his job as well. After the team got off to a slow start in 1975–76, Scott was fired.

Scott's replacement was Herb Brown, who offended most of the players with his cranky disposition. Brown did lead the Pistons to a winning record in 1976–77, but he was fired after the next season. The Pistons then slumped badly, and the club hired and fired a series of coaches. Lanier was traded to Milwaukee in 1979, and the team staggered to a 16–66 record in 1979–80. The Pistons needed to be completely rebuilt, and that rebuilding would begin with the 1981 college draft.

Rookie star Terry Tyler.

ISIAH—THERE'S NO DOUBTING THIS THOMAS

Detroit had the second pick in the 1981 draft and used it to take 20-year-old Isiah Thomas, a 6-foot-1 point guard. Thomas had led Indiana University to the NCAA championship during his sophomore season. He then decided he had nothing more to prove at the college level, so he turned pro. Detroit fans expected the little guard to lead the team to the NBA title, just as he had driven Indiana to the collegiate championship. Pistons officials, too, felt that Isiah had the ability to carry them to a league championship.

"I believe God made people to perform certain acts," said Will Robinson, Detroit's assistant general manager. "Frank Sinatra was made to sing. Jesse Owens was made to run. And Isiah Thomas was made to play basketball." Detroit coach Scotty Robertson was more than willing to give Thomas control of the Pistons on the court. "Isiah is going to do whatever needs to be done to get the job done," Robertson explained.

Thomas, however, knew that his job wasn't going to be an easy one. "I have to know every single thing about our basketball team and about each basketball player," Thomas said. "How fast he runs, and whether he shoots better on the right side or the left. If a guy gets into a rhythm, I have to be able to distribute that basketball right into his rhythm."

Thomas and rookie forward Kelly Tripucka led the team to a 39–43 record in 1981–82, an 18-win improvement over the previous season. Thomas averaged 17 points and 7.8 assists per game. Tripucka, who scored 21.6 points per game, finished second to New Jersey Nets forward Buck Williams in the voting for NBA Rookie of the Year. "Isiah and I aren't

Kevin Porter's 1,099 assists put him on top of the NBA standings for the season.

Bill Laimbeer grabs another rebound (pages 18–19).

John Long was the Pistons' top scorer, averaging 21.9 points per game.

used to losing," said Tripucka, who played his college ball at Notre Dame. "We'd like to create an atmosphere here like we had in college."

It took awhile to create that winning feeling, however. Tripucka missed 24 games during the 1982–83 season, and the Pistons missed the playoffs again. Scotty Robertson was fired after the season and replaced by Chuck Daly. Daly and general manager Jack McCloskey started to build a team that could contend for an NBA title. Thomas keyed the offense, and powerful center Bill Laimbeer was one of the best rebounders in the league. Reserve guard Vinnie Johnson added a lot of firepower off the bench. Known as the "Microwave" because of his ability to get hot fast, Johnson was capable of scoring a point a minute.

After the Pistons were beaten by the Atlanta Hawks in the

Kelly Tripucka, a scoring threat.

first round of the 1985–86 playoffs, Daly delivered a message to Detroit fans. "I hope you won't get discouraged," he said. "We are going to accomplish something this franchise has never had—an NBA championship."

Daly believed his team had the ability to be a champion. In addition to Thomas, Laimbeer, and Johnson, the Pistons had the talents of guard Joe Dumars and forward Dennis Rodman. Both were outstanding defensive players. Dumars was a better shooter and more of an offensive threat than Rodman, but Rodman, the skinny forward with the spider-like arms, was rapidly becoming one of the best defenders in the league. He was usually asked to guard the opposing team's best offensive player, perhaps Larry Bird one night and Michael Jordan the next.

Isiah Thomas put on a one-man show, scoring 16 points in only 94 seconds in a play-off loss to New York.

His powerful defense allowed Rodman to move into the starting lineup. Coach Daly loved defense. He demanded that all the Pistons work hard and always be ready to help out a teammate who had been beaten. To opponents, it was as though Detroit had seven men on the court because the Pistons always seemed to be able to double-team the ball. As many as three Pistons might be near the player with the ball. Detroit's tenacious defense was its key, but the team still needed more offensive power.

In an effort to get more scoring punch, the Pistons traded Tripucka and center Kent Benson to Utah for forward Adrian Dantley, a two-time NBA scoring champ. But Dantley and Thomas didn't click, and the Pistons got off to a slow start in 1986–87. The team soon pulled together, however, and won 52 games that season. Detroit won two playoff series, and

Reserve guard Vinnie Johnson.

then advanced to the Eastern Conference championship round against the Boston Celtics.

The two teams split the first four games of the series, setting up a crucial game five in Boston. In that game, the Pistons had a one-point lead and the ball with five seconds left. Fans in Boston Garden started to file out because the game appeared to be over. But Larry Bird stole Thomas's inbounds pass and tossed it to Dennis Johnson, who scored the game-winning layup. The Pistons ended up losing the series in seven games.

The following season, Detroit won its first-ever Central Division title with a 54–28 record. The team advanced all the way to the 1987–88 NBA championship series, but lost the league championship to the Los Angeles Lakers after a tense seven-game series. The Pistons returned to Detroit disappointed, but they knew they were closer to their goal of bringing a league crown home to Detroit.

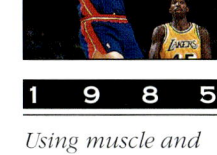

Using muscle and positioning, Bill Laimbeer led the NBA in rebounds.

WITH DUMARS, THE PISTONS WILL NOT BE DENIED

To win an NBA title, Detroit needed someone to step forward on offense and take some of the load off Isiah Thomas. That someone proved to be guard Joe Dumars, who had been playing in Thomas's shadow throughout his career in Detroit. Dumars came to the Pistons as a first-round draft pick in 1985. He had been a college star at little-known McNeese State in Louisiana, and left the school as the eleventh-leading scorer in NCAA history. But the Pistons didn't draft him to be a scorer. They wanted Dumars to be a backup playmaker to Thomas.

Adrian Dantley became only the 12th NBA player to score 20,000 points in his career.

"I wanted to score, but that wasn't what the Pistons needed," Dumars recalled. "There was just no room for me to step in and score the way I had in college. I saw they needed a defensive player, so I focused on that as a rookie. That was when I realized it might take a little longer than I had planned before I got to do all the things in the NBA I knew I could do."

By the time the 1988–89 season began, the Pistons were ready for Dumars to do everything he could. He was no longer considered just a good defensive player. He scored. He passed the ball almost as well as Thomas did. And he played defense as well as any player in the league. "What really burns me is that they talk about all the other guards in this league and never mention his [Dumars's] name," Thomas complained. "But Joe is one of the best guards in this league."

Dumars scored almost as many points a game as Thomas did during the 1988–89 season. He made more than 50 percent of his shots and was second on the team in assists. Once the regular season ended, the Pistons threw it into high gear, losing only two playoff games as they won the Eastern Conference title for the second straight year. In the league championship series, they again played the Los Angeles Lakers, who were looking for their third straight NBA title.

The Pistons won the first two games, both played in Detroit. Then the series shifted to Los Angeles, where Dumars shifted into overdrive. During the third quarter of game three, Detroit's "other guard" scored 17 points in a row for the Pistons. "Dumars wouldn't miss," recalled a stunned Mitch Kupchak, Los Angeles assistant general manager. "We kept waiting for him to miss. You could feel the whole building waiting. But it was as if he had forgotten how. He was scary."

Detroit swept the series in four straight games. Dumars, who averaged 27.3 points per game and shot 58 percent from the field, was named Most Valuable Player (MVP) of the series.

Joe Dumars was no longer underrated, and neither were the Pistons. They rolled to another league title in 1989–90. This time, Isiah Thomas was the star as Detroit defeated Portland four games to one for the league championship. Thomas averaged 27.6 points per game and was named series MVP. Vinnie Johnson wrapped up the series by hitting a last-second 15-footer to win game five.

Relentless forward John Salley led the Pistons with 137 total blocked shots for the season.

OUT WITH THE OLD, IN WITH GRANT HILL

Detroit fans hoped that the Pistons' run of titles would go on for a while. Instead, it came to a crashing halt during the 1991 playoffs, when the Pistons came up against the Chicago Bulls and their star, Michael Jordan, in the Eastern Conference Finals. The Pistons didn't give up easily against Chicago, but the series showed that Detroit had gotten a little old. The younger, hungrier Bulls outran and outhustled the aging Pistons. It was clearly time to rebuild the Motor City engine to return it to championship form.

But rebuilding became a task that ate up most of the early 1990s. While Thomas and Laimbeer were setting individual and team records, Detroit kept losing games. Dumars and Rodman—who had taken over as team leaders—were playing the best basketball of their careers, but they couldn't do

Grant Hill, the Pistons' leader (pages 26–27).

1991

Dennis Rodman earned his second consecutive honor as NBA Defensive Player of the Year.

it all on their own. The 1992–93 Pistons lost more games than they won, and failed to make the playoffs for the first time in 10 years.

Detroit's real rebuilding didn't begin until 1994, when several key moves took place. An unhappy Rodman was traded to the San Antonio Spurs, and Laimbeer—the Pistons' all-time top rebounder—retired. After a 20–62 season, Thomas—Detroit's all-time leader in points scored, assists, steals, and games played—decided to call it quits, too. That left Detroit with one player from their championship seasons—Joe Dumars. But Dumars wasn't alone for long. In the 1994 draft, Detroit picked forward Grant Hill, who had led Duke to consecutive NCAA championships. He would become the Pistons' backbone.

In his first season, Hill emerged as the team's leading scorer, showing his all-around abilities by finishing second in both assists and rebounds and third in blocked shots. Hill was co-Rookie of the Year (sharing the award with Dallas rookie Jason Kidd). Surprising everyone, Hill became the first rookie ever to lead the voting for the All-Star game, beating out Michael Jordan.

Emerging along with Hill was guard Allan Houston, who led the Pistons in scoring in 13 of their last 21 games. The Pistons won only 28 times, but in the off-season they brought in Doug Collins as the head coach, hoping he would turn Detroit's raw talent into a victorious team. Collins didn't disappoint, coaching his team to 18 more victories than the year before. Hill continued his rise to the top of the NBA, leading the league in triple-doubles, and again leading his team in points, assists, and rebounds.

"He shows up and he goes hard," said Dumars of his teammate. "He has an impact on the game every time he steps out there. He is going to continue to be great for the next 10 years. The best is yet to come."

Hill again beat Jordan in All-Star voting, while Houston continued to prove his worth, earning a reputation as a sharpshooter from three-point range. Though the Pistons lost to Shaquille O'Neal and the Orlando Magic in the first round of the playoffs, they were a team on the rise.

Free agency, however, slapped the Pistons hard when Houston signed with the Knicks before the 1996–97 season. The unexpected loss left Detroit with extra money, and they used that money to acquire Grant Long from the Atlanta Hawks, giving the Pistons a new look, and Collins a new task. "We added a couple of very strong veteran players, but

Doug Collins led the Pistons to the playoffs in his first year as head coach.

Allan Houston, a standout shooter.

Veteran leader Joe Dumars.

The smooth-scoring Grant Long.

1997

Starting out strong, rookie Jerome Williams had five rebounds in a game against the Chicago Bulls.

we have a different team right now," said Collins. "So I'm trying to build the team in a different way."

Dumars stepped up and provided veteran leadership for the new-look Pistons. "I feel much fresher now than I did the last couple of years," said Dumars in response to critics who claimed he was on the decline. "I'll just let my actions speak for me."

Dumars, Hill, and their new teammates continued to show improvement during the 1996–97 season, and much of the credit rightly went to Coach Collins, who was able to keep the new-look Pistons team on the road to the top. The Pistons were clearly a team playing hard night after night, and fans hope that the experience the players gained from working together will be the final element that makes their rise to the top of the NBA a quick and bountiful trip.

HILLTOP ELEM. LIBRARY
WEST UNITY, OHIO